CITY LIMITS

THE SCAM

ORCHARD BOOKS

96 Leonard Street, London EC2A 4RH

Orchard Books Australia

14 Mars Road, Lane Cove, NSW 2066

ISBN 1 86039 405 1 (hardback)

ISBN 1 86039 480 9 (paperback)

First published in Great Britain 1997

First paperback publication 1997

Text © Bernard Ashley 1997

A CIP catalogue record for this book is available from the British Library.

Printed in Great Britain.

Bernard Ashley

CITY LIMITS

THE SCAM

ORCHARD BOOKS

Chapter One

Drizzle ran down the plate glass of Renny's City Limits Café. The inside was clouded up with *espresso* steam and damp spirits. It was one of those miserable Friday evenings, when even Renny himself leant on his counter with his chin in his hands. He had the deli to do out, but he couldn't push himself to start.

"Ren, you look like I feel!" Sharon told him.

There was no answer to that.

"Just hold it there, Poppa," Dean said. "Art homework – sketch the look of a clogged-up cow in a cloudburst..."

Renny grunted. Why encourage cheeky sons by smiling?

But it wasn't Art homework that was drizzling on Dean, Sharon and Kwai. It was English Lit – Shakespeare, *A Midsummer Night's Dream*. Mrs Broom wanted them to learn a speech. "Commit it to memory," she'd told them.

"I dunno about memory, I could commit it to the rubbish heap, with much more of this *learnin'*!" Sharon went on. "She's filling my brain of so much Shakespeare, I've run out of room for thinking normal things..."

"Like what?" Renny was daft enough to ask.

"Like, choosing between a Coke an' a Lilt," she said. Which Renny had walked into.

He unstuck his elbow from the counter and put a few cans on a tray.

Renato Romita ran the City Limits Café, a sandwich bar with all-day breakfasts and pick-me-up teas for office workers and for people on their way to trains from City East Mainline. But around six o'clock things went quiet, and his son Dean and his friends were always welcome to one of his marble-top tables.

And the marble top tonight was covered with photocopies of Shakespeare's deathless words.

"If there *was* such a thing as a space machine, I'd want to go back in time and meet this man," Kwai said – between the murmuring and staring ahead as words tried to get printed onto memory.

"I'd go back with you, little sistuh," said Sharon. "An' I'd make him an offer he couldn't refuse – *not* to write this stuff."

Dean read the lines off his sheet, saying the piece aloud with nodding, as if that would force it in.

"*I know a bank whereon the wild thyme blows,*
Where oxlips and the nodding violet grows —"

"I know a bank wherein they bounce my mum's giros," Sharon said, as the drinks came; an excuse to clear some space of Shakespeare paper.

"No Mack tonight?" Renny asked.

Dean looked up at the KitKat clock on the wall. "He weren't at school," he said.

"*Wasn't,*" Renny corrected.

"What I said —" Had his dad traded in his brain for a parrot's? — "he weren't at school."

"*There sleeps Titania some time of the night,*"
Kwai was going for it again.

"*Lull'd in these flowers with dances and delight —*"
Stopped by Sharon. "So, what sort of a name is that? *Titania?*" — into her Lilt. "If I'm

cut back to 'Sha' what sort of a nickname does that give *her*?"

Well, they could get a smile out of it, couldn't they? It beat staring like sad cases out at the wet stuff.

The all-day breakfast regular, who always came in for his chukkie egg, bacon and two sausages, looked over at the homework table.

"I done all that Shakespeare," he dribbled, ketchup on his knife, a touch of *Macbeth*. "Still remember it.

"*Double, double, toil and trouble,*
Something something something bubble."

He tapped his forehead with his finger. "It never leaves you..."

Sharon gave him a whoop. "You're a credit to your old school, you are..."

But before she could really sizzle Chukkie's bacon, something wet suddenly blew in through the door.

It was Mack; the absent Mack, in a sodden shirt and a wide, wild-eyed state, looking "somewhere else" altogether.

"Mack!" Dean said. "What's up, mate? Lost your homework sheet?" But his voice tailed off as he took in the full strength of Mack's agitated look.

"Stuff homework sheets!"

"Agreed."

Mack looked round all their faces, helpless. "I've lost my Auntie Pearl," he said.

Mack lived with his Auntie Pearl. Three years before, when his mum had left, Mack's sisters had gone to different aunts, the baby had gone to Barnardo's, and big Jim to a merchant navy training ship. So, why him to Auntie Pearl?

Mack reckoned it was her view that he'd

been born at the age of eight, in his clothes, ready to run a message. She'd picked him because he was like a little old man in his junior school mac, and hadn't she always wanted a little old man to go round the corner shop for her, and to switch over the telly, and shut the door on the draught?

A "right hand" little old man. She was forever wanting to know, "Where's my habit?" as if she'd lost her soul instead of just her cigs. And Mack always knew – plus where she'd stuffed the Benefits book, or that other shoe, or when she'd last had her tablets. She was heavy on make-up, light on sleep, late on nights and early for pub opening. That was Auntie Pearl. But she kissed him like printing something on him – which Mack said showed she loved him, didn't it? And they rubbed along a treat.

Now it was Kwai who was first to her feet.

Others could be quick at opening their mouths, but she needed some beating at *doing* something.

"Where did you last see her?"

She brought Mack over to the table and slid a chair under him, twisting her drinks straw his way.

"I shout ta-ta yesterday morning, an' go a'school, don' I?"

Nods.

"She shouts back, suthink about being nice to the teachers… an' when I get 'ome, who's not there, but 'er?"

Dean slid him a Coke of his own, from Renny's hand. "But she's not always there, is she?"

"No, not five o'clock, six o'clock, seven o'clock, all that. Not always. Not eleven o'clock, twelve, some nights…"

"No…"

"But she don' *not kip* there. Ever. She's always in *sometime*."

Dean knew that. Mack and Auntie Pearl lived in Nelson Court, an old-fashioned block of open-balcony flats done up like Canary Wharf; with a securicom down at the main entrance, for buzzing and calling into. He'd slept over at Mack's and they'd let her in, late, when she'd lost her key: kidding her to give them the password, a test as good as a breathalyser at one a.m.

"And she's not there again today?"

"Nope."

"No note, no change of address?" As if she'd ever move on without Mack.

"Nope."

"Mack —" Sharon took his face in her hands, like Grandma Moses — "she'll come trailin' back, baby." She looked him in the eye so as to keep him taking this in. "She's gone off on a trot like an ol' pussycat, an' same as an ol' pussycat, she'll come trotting back."

"Oh, yeah, no doubt," Mack said. He nodded. "No doubt." He was brewing up with something else important, though.

"But . . . ?" asked Dean.

"But we got a problem." Mack lowered his voice till Chukkie over there nearly fell off his stool trying to earhole. "Next door. If she ain't there nights, you know what they're gonna do...?"

Dean did. He'd seen them, heard them going on at Mack and Auntie Pearl; a miserable pair without any kids who thought they owned Nelson Court. *And* they knew Mack's place in the system.

"They'll bell Social Services," Dean said.

"They'll get me took away," said Mack.

And no drizzle or *espresso* steam could cover the fact that there were tears in the poor old boy's eyes.

Chapter Two

Mack called the pair next door the Up-the-Fronts. They were up the front for everything. When Nelson Court had had a couple of beanos to the sea, who were first for front seats on the coach? The Up-the-Fronts, giving the elbow to a disabled girl so they could be first up the steps. When the water had all been turned off and a stand-pipe set up in the court, who were there first for the turning on, with bigger plastics than anyone else? The

Up-the-Fronts. And who were there eye-balling when the law came a'thumping at any of the doors? The Up-the-Fronts.

Mack just hoped that when the end-of-the-world queue for Down Below was being lined up, they'd be up the front of that, too.

Their real name was Johnson. His first name was "Mr" and her first name was "Mrs" – they never got familiar, not even being next door. And it was Mack's and Auntie Pearl's bad luck that their two living rooms backed on to one another. So when Auntie Pearl fancied a late night movie there'd be a wallop on the wall to say she was keeping their goldfish awake.

Long-nosed miseries, they were. They saw all the comings and goings in Nelson Court. Their shrivelled little eyes and cat's-backside mouths screwed up at everything that happened, from a dog cocking its leg to a coffin being shunted down the stairs. And they knew all right who called on Auntie Pearl once every three months – Dave Booty, the Social Worker. They knew that Mack, who was on the Care Register, had to be checked out from time to time.

They cornered Dave Booty when they could, jumped him on the stairs and asked how "the boy" was doing – as if they cared. And then went on about how hard it must be for an older woman to look after such a lively lad, her being *none too special* herself.

Up to now they hadn't got much change out of Dave; he'd drag his lame foot up the stairs and wouldn't let them hold him up for fear he lost his push. But Mack knew he'd have to stop and listen if they told him Auntie Pearl had done a runner; gone off on a binge.

He told the others all this while he got a doughnut down, sugar all over his face.

"See – I'm dead scared they're gonna come out on the landing an' ask me, straight. 'Where's your auntie, then?'" He did a good take-off of Mrs Up-the-Front with all her hoity toity. "An' what if I can't give 'em a good answer? They're gonna start 'otting that phone line to Social Services."

Dean had been giving it some brainpower, Shakespeare pushed well to one side. His face had the look on it which goes with someone clicking their fingers, on a roll.

"Right, so it's a two-pronged attack," he said.

Sharon made the sign of the two prongs for the Up-the-Fronts.

"First, we make the Johnsons think that your Auntie Pearl's still in the flat…"

Mack was already shaking his head.

"And, next, we find Auntie Pearl."

"Don' forget prong three," said Mack.

"Come an' visit me down the 'Ome."

"No, Mack," said Kwai, patting his hand, "we're going to help. We're going to conquer."

"An' I'll conk 'er when I see 'er," Mack said. "What game's she up to?"

"I told you, she'll come toddling home," Sharon chimed. "Meantime, we'll have a real boogaloo doing the biz on your old Johnsons. I love a good scam."

"'Ow we gonna do a scam? Jus' tell me that."

"Right," said Dean, commander of this crack team of undercover agents. "How do people know other people are indoors?"

Mack gave it some brain juice. "They see 'em," he said.

"See 'em." Dean borrowed Kwai's hand – a sharpish look from Sharon – to lift one of her fingers for counting. "And...?"

"They hear them," Kwai volunteered.

Dean went to lift another of Kwai's fingers, but Sharon got in first; except, Dean went in and lifted the third straight after. "Hear them through the wall, *and* hear them on the dog..."

"Dog?" asked Kwai.

"Dog an' bone – phone." Mack gave a pitying smile at her ignorance. "Rhyming slang." But he was looking a shade happier all round. "You reckon we can pull some stunt?" he asked Dean.

"Reckon? I definitely *do* reckon."

"Stoneginger!" said Sharon.

"No in-and-out about it," said Kwai.

"In-and-out?"

"Doubt," she told Mack. "Don't you *know* your own rhyming slang?"

Auntie Pearl's front door faced the Johnsons' across a small landing. Looking out, you saw the stairs on your left and the balcony on your right, a shared job running along both flats, with about a metre of space between the windows and the railings. And a good view across the court when there wasn't any washing out.

But, front doors facing each other! That was the killer. It was *untrue* how many times a day the Johnsons had to put milk bottles out; about as many times as there were rings on Auntie Pearl's bell. There wasn't an 'in' or 'out' they missed. And as for Auntie Pearl shaking it all about...

A nosiness Dean was counting on, in Plan A of the first prong of attack.

It was all high tech security round the flats these days. Downstairs, where the entrance was, the old open archway of shiny brown tiles was filled-in with a modern red and black metal gateway. Being Nelson Court, they'd given it the nautical touch – as if it weren't the likes of Auntie Pearl and Mack up above but Captain Bligh and Jolly Jack Tar. On the front of these fancy ironwork ropes and portholes was a push-button entry system, each flat with its own code for opening the gate.

That, or you pressed "caller" and the number of the flat you wanted – and hoped Concorde wasn't going over when you skinned your ears to hear the reply.

Tonight, Dean just wanted in, without the Johnsons seeing him. But he needed to be sure they weren't out.

Standing in under the overhang, out of the rain, Mack gave him the key to his front door, up on the third balcony. As usual, nothing was straight and easy.

"You 'ave to, sort of, take the door by surprise," Mack said. "Don' let your key dwell in the lock or it won't open."

"Oh, cheers!"

"If you can't handle it, Big Boy, I'll go!" Sharon volunteered.

"Huh!" Dean gave her his withering look; which would have had more cred if he hadn't just dropped the key in a puddle.

"Come on – give me five minutes. Got that newspaper?"

Kwai gave him last week's damp *City Echo*. This was his "cover" if the Johnsons came out – he'd deliver it to Mack's flat and come back down.

"My bit first!" said Sharon. "Stand back for a Gala Performance!"

The rest fell quiet round the push buttons. Inside, their stomachs fizzed like shaken champagne. It was like waiting for a classroom clock to tick up to the top of the hour.

"What's their number?"

"Twenny-four. No, that's mine. Twenny-five."

Sharon pushed "caller" and the "two" and "five" buttons. She cocked her ear at the little grille.

Very fast – people like the Up-the-Fronts were always on the button – a crackly raspberry came back. Then, "Yes?" Impatient as hell.

"Good evenin', madam, sorry to disturb you. We're doin' a survey on baked beans; giving away free cans for those who partake..."

Dean turned away. *Baked beans!?*

But the Up-the-Fronts would be up the front for any freebies. "What sort of survey?"

"You jus' answer a simple question..." Sharon was really getting in to this. Her face was all earnest.

"Get cut off!" Dean hissed. "They're in, that's all we need to know."

But getting cut off from a bit of fun was never Sharon's game. "One little question, then we come back next week with your free cans of baked beans."

"What's the question?" It was the man this time, up the front with the best if it meant something for nothing.

"The question is –" Sharon looked so serious. Kwai looked puzzled; Dean looked cheesed; Mack looked worried, but was holding himself ready for the laugh he knew was going to come.

"When you eat baked beans, does Crosse and Bakewell make you more flat-ul-ent, or not so – *windy* – than Heinz 57?"

There was a moment's silence from up there.

Down below, Mack burst and Kwai's eyes opened wide.

Dean turned away, thumping the wall.

"No...!"

But the weird thing was, the Up-the-Fronts went for it. "I'd never... do... such a thing personally," said the woman, "but my husband says..." They were conferring. "He'd like to try a few cans of each and let you know."

"Thank you. Answers on a postage stamp, please."

Which was such a great laugh that they had to huddle in under the overhang, in case the Johnsons twigged and looked down to see who the little monkeys were tonight. They gave it a few minutes for Sharon to stop wobbling and yooping.

"Right," said Dean, back where he'd started with Mack's key. "That's set me up a treat, that has! Wish me luck."

"Yeah, good luck, son."

"Do it quiet."

"Course."

"Not like Mr Johnson!" Which nearly had them off again, but Dean tapped in Mack's entry number and slid through the gates, *City Echo* at the ready.

"Five minutes!" he said.

"Syncopate watches," said Mack.

"And, go!" said Sharon.

Chapter Three

The stairs were concrete, so Dean didn't have to do the edge-of-the-treads job he did at home when he nipped down for something naughty from the fridge. Here at Nelson Court he skipped on his toes up and round three flights, and came to the dead potted plant which signposted Auntie Pearl's landing.

He put his eyes round the brickwork, a quick check. All clear.

And so was the Johnsons' doorstep. No

milk bottles. Outside Mack's there was one with a note in, but outside the Johnsons', nothing. They'd no doubt got them lined up inside ready for putting out at the first alert.

With the key hot in his hand, Dean walked like a paper boy to the door, taking great care not to scuff his feet. But moving fast – and keeping his eyes fixed on the Johnsons' door for any sign of a crack appearing.

He could hear a television coming out with the end of *Coronation Street*. And a sudden icicle dug into his brain. What if the telly were coming from Mack's place? What if Auntie Pearl *was* in? What would she say at Dean letting himself through the door with Mack's key?

But, worse than that. What if she was in and she *didn't* say anything? What if she was lying all still on the floor, or sitting up like a dummy in a chair? What if she'd come home ill and was in there with her clogs popped?

The thought of which made being seen by the Johnsons the skinniest of Dean's worries. He eyed up the lock, slipped in the key, took the door by surprise before it had time to think, and – to the sound of a thumping heart and a lung-full let out with a burst – he stood on the doormat (Beware of the Cat) and listened.

Nothing. Well, a clock; the fridge; *next door's* telly.

He crept into the living room. Please God let there be no one in here.

And there wasn't. Then into the kitchen. Another zero. The bedrooms – hers tidy, the other, Mack's usual wreck; and no body on either bed. Just the bathroom, which had its door closed.

Dean knocked on it. He waited in case there was a grunt or a groan, but – nothing all over again. With his heart on his tongue, he pushed it open.

Empty. Like his belly was of guts. Shower curtain drawn open, and no body in the bath, either. So, it was back to the hallway – and wait.

Their idea of five minutes seemed more like a double of English Lit. But, crouching in the hall, at last he heard their voices, loads of loud talk. Mack, Sharon, and Kwai – louder than the rest, love her.

He scuttled back into the living room and cleared his throat to get his voice ready.

Outside, Mack gave the milk bottle a good loud kick.

"Bovver!" He picked it up and put it back, for Sharon to accidentally give it one over again.

"Silly ol' me!"

The next milk bottle was from over the

way. Mrs Johnson was putting hers out by feel while she eye-balled the kids.

Mack rang at the bell. "Auntie Pearl! Auntie!" He looked over at Mrs Johnson. "Only forgot me key!" Another ring at his door. "Aunt-ie!"

Mrs Johnson quizzed up at him from doorstep level.

Behind Mack, the door opened.

"Is that you, Walter?" Dean did the Auntie Pearl, high and trill. "You left your key, you silly little monkey. Come in, son."

Mrs Johnson shifted to get a better view. But she couldn't see past the doubled-over Sharon.

"*Walter*? I forgot his name was *Walter*." It looked like she was going to die. But her voice had sounded very *baked beans lady*. She should have kept her trap shut.

"Here! Have you lot been playing about on

the intercom?" Mrs Johnson was up as straight as Big Ben. "A load of rude talk?"

"No, we've just come," said Kwai.

"But there were some kids down there," said Mack. "Playin' up again?"

Sharon was just getting her face back straight.

"Don't give me all that, boy! I want a word with your Auntie Pearl!"

No! She was coming across.

"Tea-time!" trilled Dean. "Fish fingers and –" He wanted to say baked beans but didn't want to blow it. "Come in, Walter, and all your little friends…"

They fell over themselves to get in and get the door shut before Mrs Johnson could make it.

The woman stood on the landing and stared at the shut door, before she turned and went back to her own flat. With a look on her face which said something was definitely going on over the way.

The sort of look she had on when she was going to be up the front for trouble.

Chapter Four

Dean looked a treat in Auntie Pearl's Chinese dressing gown and floral shower cap. With the silky collar pulled up and the plastic pulled down, there wasn't a lot of face to be seen. Just the mouth, really, which Kwai attended to with a ruby-red lipstick, the best bit for Dean.

Mack said he fancied him. So they could all tell that Mack wasn't feeling *dire* about Auntie Pearl. There was every chance she was coming round somewhere, Alka Seltzer and a ciggie to help, moaning on about who'd put wicked *drink* in her drink? It was the fact of her not being there, and the Up-the-Fronts reporting it to the Social that worried Mack.

The heads-and-tails of which was, they needed one more go at making everything seem normal up there on the third landing. They'd ruled out any idea of "Auntie Pearl" phoning through to next door as being too risky.

But Sharon had hit on it; well, she needed to, after being the one who'd opened the door to doubt with too much old talk.

"Now, listen good. Mack goes over there an' asks for the lend of something for tea, what with all us bein' here —"

"Not a tin of baked beans?" Dean put to her.

He unstuck himself from the wall, rubbing his head.

"*Real* funny. A drop of milk, Doze, or a couple o' tea bags. An' "Auntie Pearl" is stood well back here in the passage, an' she shouts "Thank you!" or "Up yours!" according to what they say. Important thing is, they get a quick look at her..."

"Sounds good," said Kwai.

"Well, thank you, sistuh."

"But what if they come over, or start up talking?"

"Right!" said Sharon, clicking her fingers as it came. "Thought of that." She was on a roll. "That's when you dial that number, the one that makes your own phone ring – soon as there's any danger. An' "Auntie Pearl" says, 'Gotta go, it's the—'"

"Dog and bone," said Kwai. Proudly.

Mack grinned and hugged Kwai – when, to be fair, Sharon should have had the acclaim.

"Right, then," said Dean. "Let's do it, quick.

Else I might smudge my lipstick…"

"Wanna come dancing, Sat'day night?" asked Mack, with a pout. For which he got a slap round the face.

He opened the front door and went across the landing as if it were a minefield. Kwai stood in the living room doorway with the phone. Dean stood a metre or so back in the passage with Sharon near, who was ready to come in front of him if the Johnsons made any sort of rush.

Knock-knock.

"Yes?" Mrs Up-the-Front had the sort of grouchy face on like a bloodhound's.

"Sorry to disturb you –"

"Which you have!" But not so out of sorts that she couldn't try to look over Mack's shoulder at the other doorway.

"Yoo-hoo! All right, dearie?" Dean waved to her.

"We got my mates round, so, er, Auntie there says, could you give 'er a lend of a cup o' milk. Till the morning."

He might as well have been asking for a mention in the woman's will.

"Definitely not! And I want a word with your auntie..." Already, Mrs Johnson was bending to jam the mat in the door.

"She's coming out!" hissed Sharon. "She's coming over!"

"Whoa!" from a shaky Dean.

"Dial! Dial!" Sharon pushed Kwai.

While Mrs Johnson brushed Mack aside and took the first of three steps which would have her on Auntie Pearl's runner.

"*Dial!*" Sharon spun round to help, but the phone was the wrong way round, and anyway she knocked the thing out of Kwai's hand with a crash and a pathetic little ping.

"Harken! There goes the phone!" trilled

Dean, and turned to go. And it was just bad luck that he caught his heel in the hem of Auntie Pearl's dressing gown and got yanked back to fall flat on the floor, two long hairy legs and a pair of Juventus boxers waving up at Mrs Johnson.

Mack just about went through Mrs Johnson to get indoors first, slamming the door, eye in the peep hole to see the woman standing staring in a mild case of shock.

"She'll be all right," he told her through the door. "I'll give 'er a drop of her camembert tea."

And the four of them froze while Mrs Johnson went on standing there, still staring. Pondering.

The problem being, people who always get themselves up the front for everything are never anybody's fools.

Chapter Five

Homework would have to wait. Saturday was Prong Two day. Never mind *A Midsummer Night's Dream*, now they had to find their midsummer night's runaway, Auntie Pearl.

And the best bet for starting was round at the *Samuel Pepys*, the City East local where Auntie Pearl took her custom. It had a theatre upstairs, but she didn't go for that. Downstairs in the saloon bar they served her favourite London gin, and for her, Micky Dunn the

Irish barman always gave good measure.

Plus, the regular fellows made a fuss of her, as if she were still twenty, or thirty, or forty – and "Who minds a little bit of being treated special?" she always said.

It was the sort of place where they wore jackets or ironed shirts, and their trousers could remember having a crease. And Auntie Pearl had no competition in her own age group – but she still went round dressed up for cocktail hour, her bleached hair cut in a bob and her black beaded top just lacy enough to let her Gossard show through; handling her cigs and her lighter like Princess Margaret.

The pub opened at eleven and, after the rain of the night before, it was a fine sunny morning which saw Mack and Dean crashing in at two minutes past.

Mack knew the way. Going in here for him

was like some other kid popping in to his mum's work.

Micky Dunn was still setting up, more into his coffee than the hard stuff he was putting up on the mirror shelf.

"Hi, there, Mack."

"Micky —"

"That's my name…"

Dean turned back to the door and pulled a face. Why were people so blessed *hopped up* at the crack of eleven?

"You seen Pearl anywhere?"

"Pearl?"

"Yeah, you know the one. My auntie. Thinks you're a decent bloke."

"Oh, that one!" Micky looked down behind the bar, opened the "Private" door, lifted an upturned glass. "No, Mack, she ain't here."

Dean plopped himself on a leather settee.

This sad humour could go on all day.

"What about last night?"

"That'd be – ?"

"Last night."

"No, she weren't in last night."

"An' the night before?"

"The night before?"

"*Ters*day."

"No. But she was in Tersday lunchtime. All done up, top drawer. In a rush, grabbed one o' my pork pies."

"Was she all right?"

"Well she had one o' my pork pies."

"Off 'er 'ead, then."

"Serious, though, come to think of it, she went off somewhere wi' Derek the Dog."

"Dogs don't run Thursday, do they?"

"Not local."

"So where'd she go with him?"

You could search Micky. "Somewhere in

his car, I can tell you that."

"Ow d'you know?"

"He soft-touched me for petrol money."

Dean came up to the bar. "Do you know where he lives? This Derek the Dog?"

"He rooms somewhere. Up near the station, isn't it?"

"Dunno."

"Sure, up near the station. Over the bookies."

"That'd be the touch," Mack said.

"You know what he looks like?"

"Yeah, two eyes, nose, coupla' ears..."

"That's the one."

"Cheers, Micky."

"Any time."

"Oh, I *do* hope not," said Dean as they went out.

Of course, being Saturday, there was no one answering Derek the Dog's door on the landing above the bookies. Mack knocked, and Dean knocked, to satisfy himself, but neither of their knockings got any result.

"The stable's empty," said Mack.

"Be 'kennel'," said Dean, "for Derek the Dog."

"Yeah, the dog 'as flown."

"That'd be 'bird'."

"Right. The nest is bare."

"That'd be 'cupboard'."

"An' the skelington's gone."

"Shall we just say, he's not at home?" And only then did Dean see Mack's wicked face, and know he was being jacked around rotten.

"'E's down the dogs," said Mack. "Sat'day afternoon. Propping up the punters' bar."

"You mean, he *might* be. He is the last person seen with your Auntie Pearl alive."

Which made Mack's face turn very straight. He really hadn't been thinking *seriously* gone missing. He bent to Derek the Dog's letterbox again, but he still couldn't see through the draught excluder nailed on the inside.

He took a sniff at it.

"Come on, stiffs don't go off that quick," Dean comforted him. "Let's see if Sha an' Kwai fancy an afternoon down the dogs."

"Yeah. Check downstairs that's where 'e's gone – an' one more check on the way back to your place."

"Where? Where else would he be?"

"Not 'im. 'Er."

Dean frowned.

"A&E – Casualty – better just run a check up the 'ospital."

Both of which they did. And, yes, the girl in the bookies reckoned the bloke upstairs *was* down the dogs. He was on his tod, as usual; and the car was all parked up round the back.

And, no, no one answering the description of Auntie Pearl had been admitted to the City Free. Perhaps they ought to try the police station?

But Mack wasn't having that. "Them and the Social work 'and-in-pocket, don' they?" Only on a last life-saver would he pull himself in there.

So, there'd be a meet up at City Limits Café as planned at two-ish, and off they'd go to the dogs.

But there was a touch of tension in the air. Thursday night, Friday, and this was Saturday already. It was a bit different to Auntie Pearl going missing on a shindy.

Chapter Six

Only Mack had ever been to the dogs. Before she'd gone off, his mum had dragged him along in a push chair, years ago – one of those evenings where you went everywhere backwards. So there wasn't much he could tell the rest about what it would be like.

Renny kept an eye on the kids round the table, without keeping an eye. He knew they were up to some scheme but he couldn't figure what. It was Sharon being quietish that had him on the puzzle.

He waved a handful of scruffy sheets of Shakespeare at them.

"I kept a hold on these," he said, fishing.

"Cheers, Poppa."

"You know all this, do you? *I know a bank — ?*"

"Yeah, yeah, yeah, yeah…"

"How about I test you on it?"

"This man's all heart!" Sharon told the café.

"But should we take his precious time?"

There was a general shaking of heads, including a couple of customers.

"You count your olives," Dean told him.

Whisper, whisper, huddle, huddle, followed by a quick exit – to the bus stop, and on to Victoria Dogs.

"They do economics young, don't they?" a bacon sandwich remarked. "Knowing about banks…"

"They do *everything* young," said Renny.

Which included getting in at the grey-hound track. Children and pensioners shared a cheap turnstile. Dean, Sharon, Kwai and Mack timed their entry to go in with a little cluster of punters going through the adults' door, as if they were all together, about to meet up on the inside.

"OK," said Dean, "so where are we going to find Derek the Dog?"

Mack had a scratch. The oval track stretched lengthways in front of them. On their left were the restaurant and the executive boxes, on their right the banking with the bookies and the bars. Facing them, at the other end of the stadium, was a huge screen, like a computer display of coloured numbers.

"With an 'andle like 'Derek the Dog' 'e's gonna be where the main punters are," Mack reckoned. "On that bank."

"I know a bank where the money goes," said Kwai; and would have got a little ripple for it if they hadn't wanted to keep their heads down.

As they walked round – the place wasn't crowded – the dogs were being paraded for the next race, the number one with a red bib, led by a pimply boy in a red Terylene jacket; the number two in blue, down to the number six in stripes, whose kennel maid had a white coat with felt-tip lines drawn on it.

"All a bit tat, isn't it?" Dean said.

"Not if ol' Pearl's 'ere," said Mack. "Be golden then." He was getting worried, was the boy.

They walked round to the concrete stepping where the *real* punters were; some sitting on the steps, some standing, one eye on the dogs, another on the big electronic board which showed them how the betting was going, nationwide.

Facing them from in front of the track were three bookies on little boxes, each with a Gladstone bag with his name on, and a board showing the runners and the odds. They were watching the electronics, too, as well as each other, changing the odds as their assistants on the steps shouted to them. And when a little bevy of backers suddenly ran down to get their bets on at a good price, they changed the odds again with a wipe of their sleeves and a quick squiggle on their boards.

Like a dog out of a trap, Mack suddenly left the rest. "There 'e is! Got 'im!"

He weaved himself along the steps like an Olympic walker, fast without running. All at once this was Mack's play, and his alone.

Derek the Dog was a tall man, grey-haired in an old-fashioned gelled-up style; with a small moustache, long legs, a business shirt worn open-necked, and a pair of trousers belted up under his breast. Like all the others, he had one eye on the electronics, one on the bookies' odds, and was hardly giving a look to the dogs parading round and doing their bits of business. And not for a second looking the sort who would want to hurt Auntie Pearl. Just the opposite: he looked more like he could do with a quiet cuddle.

Mack came sidling fast along the concrete step.

"Auntie Pearl," he said.

"Which race?" Derek the Dog didn't bat an eye.

"*My* Auntie Pearl."

"Who fancies her?"

"Good question!" Mack tapped his arm, hardish. Derek the Dog looked at him now.

"Oh, it's you! Walter, isn't it?"

"Yeah – an' I've lost my Auntie Pearl. You know, Pearl Collins."

"*Pearl!*" The man laughed. "Thought you was giving me a tip."

"So, where is she? Micky Dunn said—"

"Hold on!"

There was just a second of thought. And Derek the Dog suddenly lunged away from Mack, making a run.

But Mack was quick out of his trap. He was less than the split of a second behind.

"Oi! Come 'ere!' And he had the man round the waist, got himself dragged down the steps.

"Be'ave yourself!" Derek the Dog tried to shake him off.

A bell rang.

"The hare's running!" came a voice on the Tannoy. Others who had suddenly run forward came back again. The bookies jumped off their boxes and stood with the punters on the steps, watching the dogs come leaping out after the "hare" on rails.

"What's that for?" Derek the Dog finally threw Mack off, and stood there all limp and disappointed.

"Where's Pearl Collins?" Mack gritted on.

"Brighton, you dope. Gone to see her cousin. I took her to Victoria Coach Station."

"Eh?"

"You just cost me a good price on my dog. I'll flatten you if she comes in on the nose!"

But Mack was no coward. He didn't go to find Dean and the gang. He stood next to Derek the Dog, his eyes with everyone else's on the six dogs whipping round the sandy oval. He'd stay and take his medicine, if it had to come.

But there was a mighty groan, and a score of crumpled betting slips hit the steps.

"Lucky for you!" said Derek the Dog. "I wasn't doing no runner, son, I was going for a good price."

"Did you…would you 'ave won?" Mack was desperate to know.

"No, came fourth an' lost her beer money, didn't she?"

Mack's relief came out like a whale spouting. "So what's the deal with Auntie Pearl?"

Derek the Dog took time to explain; but still with one eye on the odds for the next race. How Auntie Pearl had had a phone call, her cousin was suddenly taken ill, and she was going down to the coast to see her. "Like you do if you think someone's gonna pop off sudden." And Derek the Dog had given her a lift across town.

"She said she'd left you a note."

"Didn't see it."

"Well, that's where she's gone."

"Cheers."

Mack went back to the others.

"Strewth! What was all that?" Dean asked. "We were just coming in with the heavy ammunition when it looked like you were kissing and making up."

"Good job you didn't." And Mack told them the score.

"Yeah, good job an' all!" said Sharon. She was holding a tenner in her hand. "Got someone to put a pound on number three, up at the window."

They wanted to stay after that, but finding Auntie Pearl edged it; although their heads were twisted over their shoulders as they went.

"What made you go for number three?" Kwai asked. "You know about dogs?"

"Nah!" Sharon laughed. "I bet from the heart, sistuh, not the head. It was the name, done it for me."

"What was that?" Dean was into the race card.

"'Titania's Dream'," she said. "Gotta pay off somehow, hasn't he, ol' Shakespeare?"

Chapter Seven

Mega surprise! By the time they got to Nelson Court she was back at the ranch. Auntie Pearl. They'd gone racing back to find her address book and sort out who she knew living on the south coast – and there she was herself, sitting on the sofa all tense, with the look on her face of someone still pacing up and down the room.

"Oh, poor Vi, she's not well at all," Auntie Pearl told Mack as they all came into the room. She pulled a hankie out of the sleeve of her blouse. "An' that hospital..." she dropped her voice as if Vi were here with them, hearing this... "they're not telling her everything..." A little shake of her head. It was a sad moment.

But Mack was brilliant with Auntie Pearl. He knew just how to handle her. He didn't go diving in with "Where was you? Why didn't you? 'Ow could you?" He didn't even ask her who the heck this Vi was. He let it come out, about her sick cousin, who'd been taken into Brighton General for observation.

"Her brother's come over from the Isle o' White, so I came away..."

"Right."

"She's in the best place." Auntie Pearl sighed – it comes to us all, being in the best place, and she was nearer to it than these kids.

Mack poured her a small brandy. "You've

'ad a right ol' shock, love."

"You can say that again."

And, good for Mack, he didn't; not this once. He just told her how he'd been a bit worried, not knowing where she was, but Derek the Dog had told him.

"But, I left you a note, boy." She was still fanning her face, easing her shoulder straps, looking round for her ciggies.

"Where?"

"Up there. Where else?"

She pointed to the top of the telly, where there was a note all right, half a sheet of A4 torn from Mack's Scribbling Block.

"Nah." Mack got it. "Seen that." He waved it at her. *No milk today, thank you.*

"Bli! Who's a Joker short of a full deck?" Auntie Pearl whooped, but she couldn't really get behind it, not today. "Must be the milkman who knows where I was!"

Sharon saw the funny side. "Bet he's blown you out, though. Long way to go for a drop with cream on top!"

Mack clicked his fingers. "An' I kicked that bottle to bring the Johnsons out." But he tailed it off as soon as he'd begun – he didn't want to get into all that.

And the rest tailed off out of it altogether, left him with her. Auntie Pearl needed her little old man's arm round her shoulder right now. After all, she'd just come back from a nasty reminder that no one goes on for ever.

Renny could have closed, Saturday evenings. He could have given himself a night out, except for Sophia often working so many Saturdays at her make-up job for the television; and the City Limits Café was an ace place for Dean and his friends to hang out. He let them bring their music in on Saturdays, a small price for knowing they weren't up to no good round the streets.

Instead, they were up to no good in here. Except Mack, who was missing. While Renny coloured a sketch he'd done of Kwai, Sharon was expanding her survey of baked beans into other foodstuffs and their effects on people. Like, teachers. Right now she was on about Mr Carter and onions.

"Man, the pong off of him, he's got to eat onions by the cart!"

"No, not with that dog's breath," Dean said. "He's got to eat *Chum*!"

"An' what about Mrs Primp? That stink of violets coming off her..."

"Covers the smell of brandy," said Kwai. "She takes it for the fear."

Renny looked up. Was he supposed to hear

all this, or not? Should he have a dig about showing respect for their teachers?

He twiddled his brush in the muddy paint water, and went for fresh. On the way, he came across that clutch of scruffy homework sheets.

"Homework," he said. "Have you done it?"

"You bet!" said Sharon. "Good work at Mack's home. A diff'rent sort of home-work…"

"Practical," said Kwai.

"But this learning by heart," Renny waved it at them, "how's that going along?"

They groaned, and Dean quietly added the sound of an escaped baked bean. But if his father heard it above the music, he didn't have time to go public. Because in came Mack, through the door without opening it, sort of thing.

"They've done it!" he said. "They've only done it!"

"Put a man on Mars?"

"The Up-the-Fronts! Them Johnsons!" He'd have spat if he hadn't been indoors. "They've only got on the dog to Social Services!"

"What for, Mack?" Kwai asked. "She's back, isn't she?"

Mack walked round a table three times. "For bein' two nights away. 'Is she fit an' proper?' An' my social worker's only comin' round to inspect!"

"When?"

"Now. Soon as 'e can get a fresh refill in 'is ballpoint."

"So?" But for a "so?" it didn't sound bad, not the way Dean said it, with a concerned look; not, "So what's it got to do with us?", but more, "So, what can we do to help?"

Mack was there already. "So what about we say she'd made arrangements for me to sleep round 'ere? While she was off?"

But Dean didn't need to even glance at his dad to know how much *that* wasn't on.

"Else, 'e's gonna 'ave to think she's really top ace at looking after me. Or they'll 'ave me in the 'ome, I know it."

"Well, she is, isn't she?" Sharon got very stiff-backed about any injustice. "She just had a crucial crisis, that sistuh!"

"What things will they be looking at?" Kwai wanted to know, thinking round the problem.

Renny knew, when they asked him. He came back with his pot of clean water and counted off each point with a dab on the homework. "It'll be, attending school regular and punctual, clothing, health and food, and moral upbringing."

"Well, she's taken a trip on the last one! But five out of six ain't bad!" Sharon reckoned.

"You ever met my mum?"

"It's gotta be six out o' six," Mack gloomed. "We need another dab on ol' Ren's paper."

"Top whack, she's got to be a model good parent, and a pillar of society," Dean said. He clicked his fingers. "And if she was a pillar for the rest of the youth, as well as for her Walter, that'd be a plus…"

"What you on about?"

"Come on!" said Dean. "All round Mack's, quick! I've got an idea."

"But is it any good?"

"We'll have to see. But it's your only chance," said Dean. "Have I ever let you down?"

"Yeah, when you fell over and showed your inside leg to Mrs Up-the-Front."

But, Dean didn't hear. He was halfway up the street towards Nelson Court.

Chapter Eight

Dave Booty spoke into the entry grille and was let in from above. He spoke quietly, and moved in through the gateway as if he were walking on hot sand. His lame leg made him clomp on most stairs, but tonight he gave himself the extra pain to stay silent. He'd had the Johnsons on the phone, he could do without them in living colour.

And, success, he got himself inside Pearl

Collins' front door before the Up-the-Fronts could lay hands on a clean milk bottle to put out.

"Come in, Dave," said Auntie Pearl, as if he were a long lost friend. Not a ciggie in sight, the hallway sweet and heavy with Midnight in Marrakesh. Mozart tinkled on the hi-fi through the open door of Mack's bedroom, and a framed Cézanne was still swinging into its hang on the wall.

In her hand, Auntie Pearl was holding a thickish book without its dust cover, a crooked finger keeping her place.

"I'm just giving these young people their weekly seminar."

"Seminar?"

The question wasn't dry on Dave's lips before he was in the small living room, where a group of earnest students were lounging on the chairs and the floor. They, too, had volumes like Auntie Pearl's, and pages of notes.

"Our little tutorial."

"I had hoped for a word with you on your own," Dave said.

"But come in and sit down first. You know, I'm so *proud* of these students. Friends of Walter. I offer them what I have, my background in English Lit–er–ature…"

Auntie Pearl sat down as if her flowing kimono were a university gown. "We've nearly finished, then they'll have earned their refreshment."

"Just water and a dry biscuit for me, thank you," said Sharon. "As usual." Which got a piercer from Dean.

Professor Pearl clapped her hands. "Please continue to the end of the speech. Read it round from your books," she said.

Mack dusted a chair with his hankie, and offered it to Dave.

Kwai cleared her throat, held up her volume, just the eyes showing above. "*I know a bank whereon the wild thyme blows...*"

"Next," said Auntie Pearl.

"*Where oxlips and the nodding violet grows,*" said Dean, into his own volume.

"And...?" said Auntie Pearl, conducting Sharon in with a long, smoker's finger.

"*Quite over-canopied with luscious woodbine.*" Sharon's voice was thick in her throat with holding herself in from exploding.

"*With sweet musk-roses, and with eglantine:*" Kwai came in again, to take the pressure off Mack.

"Well, yes," said Dave.

"You see, it's a precious stillness in a busy world, my little flat on a Saturday night," said Auntie Pearl. "Read on silently, all of you." She thumped her volume shut. "These youngsters, keen to learn, come in off the streets from their poor, rough backgrounds into this pool of calm."

Mack swung a look at her that cricked his neck. This was well over the top.

"I don't ever know how to thank you," Sharon said to Auntie Pearl. "All that noise with my brothers and sisters. An' three pet greyhounds racing round the table..." She drew in a breath to go on, but got a kick from Dean.

"Yes, I can see that," said Dave Booty. "If only there were more homework sanctuaries..."

"How kind of you to say."

"It's just that, well, this going off..." His voice returned to the business in hand.

But Auntie Pearl had already put her hands up. "I know. I was 'council lifts' – well out of order. A *very* sick cousin who needed help, and a cancelled train home. A travesty of errors. I thought I'd made proper arrangements, but —" a dramatic pause — "I was let down, Dave. *Let down.*" She looked in the direction of the Johnsons' flat. "Say no more!"

Dave shut his file, lugged himself to his feet. "Well, next time, ring me, Pearl. I'm your contact, I'm your social worker..." He stopped, as if it had suddenly come to him again that this *was* private stuff.

"No, speak, I've got no secrets from my keen band of learners. Spiel on."

"Well, I'm here to help, Pearl, when there's a crisis. That's my job."

"You wonderful man. *Dear* Dave."

"And I've got to run — well, do the best I can." He tucked his battered casework bag under his arm. "I've got no real problems here. There's more to you, Pearl, than meets the eye."

He looked at the seminar group. "What's the text?" he asked; suddenly swinging it round on Auntie Pearl — but not so much on purpose as slightly losing his balance.

"*A Midsummer Night's Dream*," said Mack, a shaft at light's speed.

"Lovely. Bottom, and all that, isn't it?"

"Yeah."

"Now we're back to baked beans!" grunted Sharon.

They let him get out and away, but the laugh was all the louder for being held in for the time it takes to go down a flight of stairs.

"Whoo-hoo!" whooped Sharon, high-fiving it all round the room.

"Got a result!" crowed Mack.

"I never felt so nervous!" said Kwai. She held up her heavy volume.

"I thought you all 'read' it very well," said Auntie Pearl, lighting up a ciggie on her way across to the drinks cabinet.

Dean piled the books on the table. "*The Complete Works of Shakespeare,*" he said. "Four copies. Not!" He picked up the first, and read the title from the spine. "*A Night in Old Paris.*" He picked up the next. "*Naked in the Snow*". And the next. "*Who Needs a Bed?*" And the last. "*The Man Who Lost His All*".

"My little library," said Auntie Pearl. "Collectors' items, those. *The Kiss and Tell Book Club*. Better than your old videos for a saucy yarn."

Kwai was still fanning herself. "I'm just glad he never looked over my shoulder!"

"Well, you know it, don't you? You proved you know it by heart." Auntie Pearl was sitting down again with a stiff toddy. She turned to Mack. "You'll have to catch up with them, tomorrow. Meantime, break out the pork scratchings for my top drawer students."

But Dean was on his feet. "No, got to go,"

he said. "Thanks." Crisps or peanuts, OK, but pork scratchings!

And they'd done the business. They'd helped Mack in spades by being Auntie Pearl's "students", making her look like a caring expert on old William Shakespeare.

"Yeah, I'm blowing an' all." Sharon fancied going with Dean.

"I'll hang on," said Kwai, "if that's all right."

Mack smiled. It was ten times all right with him.

Dean and Sharon got to the door.

"Oh, and when you discuss those lines from *The Dream* with your teacher —" Auntie Pearl was looking at them with eyes suddenly sharp through the cigarette smoke.

"Yeah?" Dean was lopsided, ready for a laugh to go out on.

"Don't forget that Oberon is not only

telling Puck how he will sort Titania, all fairy-land stuff, he's also wiring into the human beings' love story; so the way you say that speech has to get more *earthly* at the end..."

Dean stood while his open mouth dried out. Mack's Auntie Pearl knew more than Mrs Broom from the sounds of her.

"Get off, then – and ta, loves." She gave them a saloon bar wink.

"Our pleasure," said Sharon.

And they were on the doorstep staring across at a bottle coming out from over the way when Mack caught them up, giving the biggest victory smile possible across at the Up-the-Fronts.

"See? I won' 'ave no trouble with me Shakespeare, will I?" he said. "See you in English!"

More

City
Limits

stories...

Bernard Ashley

STITCH-UP

Dean and Sharon are an item. She's sharp, funny and beautiful. Her half-brother is sharp too – sharp and dodgy. So when a robbery takes place right in front of him, Dean has some heavy-duty thinking to do. Does his loyalty to Sharon extend to her brother? Or is this a stitch-up?

CITY LIMITS 1

Bernard Ashley

A famous face arrives at the City Limits Café – a TV face, the Big I am. He commands attention and gives stick, which rocks young Lucy's confidence on stage and off. Sharon's a natural at play acting herself, and she's up to teaching him a thing or two. So watch out Mr Big, you're about to be framed!

CITY LIMITS 3

Bernard Ashley

MEAN STREET

A runaway gets Dean and Mack in a spin. She's a kid with attitude, a fighter, a survivor. Now Mack's comfortable bed gives him sleepless nights and Dean wants to forget he ever met her. Kwai's kindness only makes things worse. So can they help, will they help, a kid down on her luck on Mean Street?

CITY LIMITS 4